TWISTERS RHYMERS

Tall Story

Christine Moorcroft and Neil Boyce

Evans

One morning, Paul was bored.

"I know," he thought,
"I'll play football."

But his shorts were torn.
His socks were worn.

"Mum – where's my ball?
I can't find it at all."

"It's in the hall," Mum called.

Out he walked
and kicked his ball.
It went into orbit.

14

He heard a call: "Goal!"

But who had scored?

Then he saw...
...giants, taller than the wall,
playing football!

They were big and brawny.

Paul felt small and scrawny.

One said, "Good morning.
Come and play!
We need a scorer."

Paul wasn't sure.
He had never seen
giant footballers before.

Then the supporters
began to call,
"Paul! Paul!"

He heard them roar.

But it was Mr Court
next door
at number four.

"He'll never believe my story," thought Paul.

Twisters Rhymers follow on from the success of the Twisters series. Twisters are gripping short stories from different genres, told in just 50 words, with an appealing choice of illustration styles and content. Why not try one?